With love to my sisters-in-AWE-someness,
Sandy and Beth
—H. B. R.

For Me-Me and Bun-Bun
—M. W.

Henry Holt and Company, *Publishers since 1866*
Henry Holt® is a registered trademark of Macmillan Publishing Group, LLC
175 Fifth Avenue, New York, NY 10010 • mackids.com

Text copyright © 2019 by Heidi Bee Roemer
Illustrations copyright © 2019 by Mike Wohnoutka

Library of Congress Cataloging-in-Publication Data
Names: Roemer, Heidi, author. | Wohnoutka, Mike, illustrator.
Title: Peekity boo! what you can do / Heidi Roemer ; illustrated by Mike Wohnoutka.
Description: First edition. | New York : Henry Holt and Company, 2019. |
Summary: Rhyming text follows a toddler's bedtime routine, from an
energetic bath to choosing jammies, reading a book, cuddling with a
favorite toy, and snuggling with loved ones before gently falling asleep.
Identifiers: LCCN 2018020979 | ISBN 9781250122322 (hardcover)
Subjects: | CYAC: Stories in rhyme. | Bedtime—Fiction. | Toddlers—Fiction.
Classification: LCC PZ8.3.R619 Pe 2019 | DDC [E]—dc23
LC record available at https://lccn.loc.gov/2018020979

Our books may be purchased in bulk for promotional, educational, or business use.
Please contact your local bookseller or the Macmillan Corporate and Premium Sales Department
at (800) 221-7945 ext. 5442 or by e-mail at MacmillanSpecialMarkets@macmillan.com.

First edition, 2019 / Design by Katie Klimowicz
The artist used acryla gouache on watercolor paper to create the illustrations for this book.
Printed in China by Hung Hing Off-set Printing Co. Ltd., Heshan City, Guangdong Province
1 3 5 7 9 10 8 6 4 2

Peekity Boo
What You Can Do!

Heidi Bee
Roemer

illustrated by
Mike
Wohnoutka

Christy Ottaviano Books
HENRY HOLT AND COMPANY • NEW YORK

Peekity boo!

Look what Baby can do . . .

There's a shirt
to slip off.

Socks to kick off.

Splishity splash!
Here's Baby's bath.

There are bubbles to pop.

Toys to kerplop!

Duck to take swimming.

Boat to take skimming.

Blibbity blub.

Bye-bye, sudsy tub.

Buggity boo!
Now what
do we do?

There are ears to nuzzle.

Towel to snuggle.

Belly to tickle.

Toesies to wiggle.

Jammies to slip in.

Chair to sit in.

Songs to sing you.

Books to look through.

Peekity boo!

Now what do we do?

Tweedle tum.

Nighttime has come.

There's milk to sip up.

Blankie to pick up.

Teddy to cuddle.

Bunny to bundle.

Star to wish on.

Cheek to kiss on.

Dreams to come true.

Hugs to give you.

Peepity peep.
Shhh . . . **Baby's asleep.**

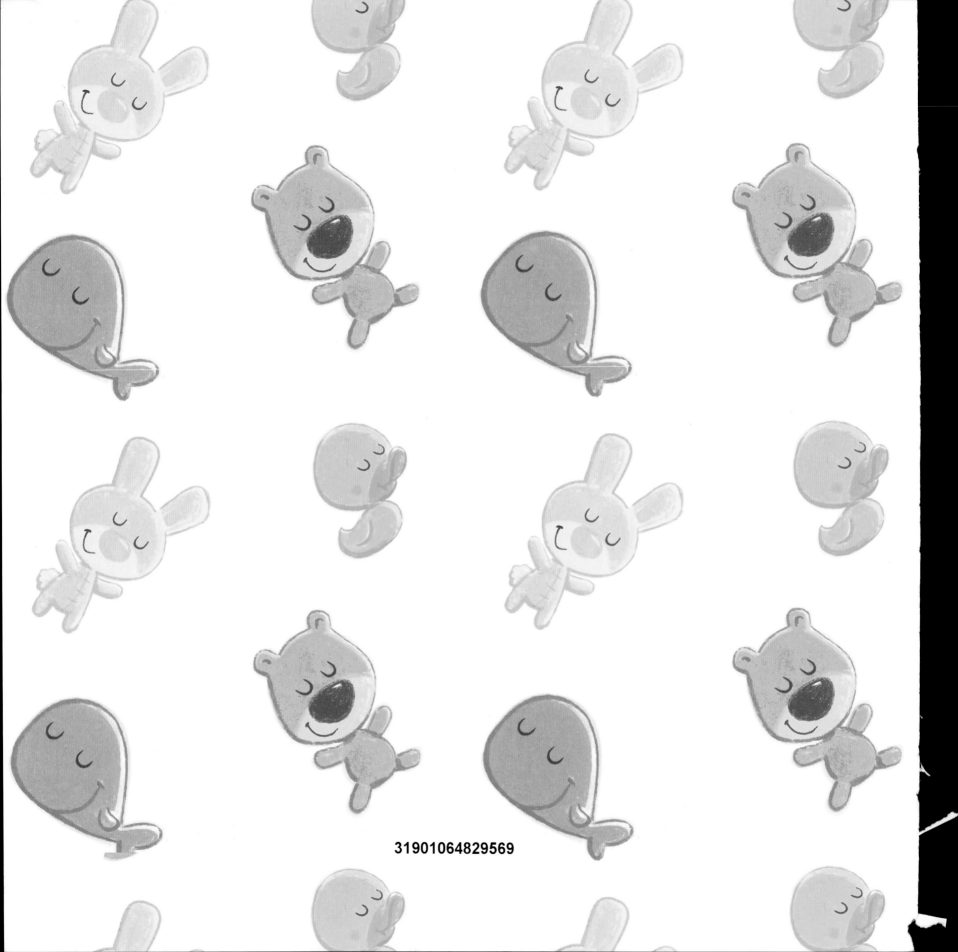